UNICORN IN NEW YORK

LOUIE
IN A
SPIN!

RACHEL HAMILTON

Illustrated by Oscar Armelles

OXFORD
UNIVERSITY PRESS

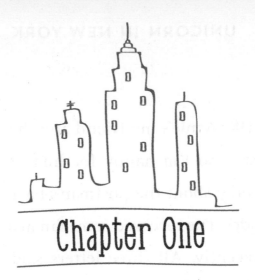

Chapter One

Unanswered Questions

Greetings, humans. Me again. Louie, your favourite unicorn. Hmmm, perhaps make that your *second* favourite unicorn. I've seen Arnie the Unicorn's massive postbag of fan mail and fluffy toys. But that's OK. Arnie's my friend and the school superstar, so I'm happy for him. Really. I just worry about the postman's back.

Besides, I've received some fan mail of my own recently. All three letters said they'd love to hear more of my adventures at the New York School for Performing Arts. So, here you go. Prepare for a tale of daring leaps and dazzling dance steps. Oh, and a few near-disasters, but we'll whizz through those.

Anyway, my tale begins in the corridor outside the school dance studio, where my friends were refusing to answer my questions.

'Hey, roomies,' I said. 'What's with the big poster on the notice board about a dance competition?'

'Hey, Louie. Did you enjoy the vegetables at lunch?' asked Danny the Faun, who'd shown no interest in green beans before.

'Er. Lovely, thanks,' I replied, wondering if Danny had bumped his head in the canteen. 'So? Miranda?' I turned to my favourite mermaid. 'Do you know anything about this dance competition?'

Miranda the Mermaid fiddled with her hair. 'Nice weather for this time of year, isn't it?'

'No.' I watched the raindrops trickle down the windows. 'Rain does horrible things to a unicorn's mane. Why are we talking about the weather? Frank, *you* tell me. What's this about a dance competition?'

'Baseball!' Frank the Troll blurted, avoiding my eyes. 'What did you think of last night's match?'

'Baseball?' I stared at Frank. 'Since when have either of us watched baseball?'

'Humans like it,' Frank muttered, scratching his armpit.

I shook my head. Why was no one listening to me? I tried one more time: 'WHAT IS THAT ON THE NOTICE BOARD ABOUT A DANCE COMPETITION?'

A small girl in a leotard, who was walking

past, stopped and grinned. 'Exciting, isn't it? Every art and dance school in the country is taking part.'

I clapped my hooves together. 'That *does* sound exciting. Why has no one mentioned it before?'

Frank and Danny whistled and Miranda did a few somersaults in her mermaid tank.

Leotard Girl stared at me open-mouthed. 'People have been talking about nothing else all week. How have you missed it? Madame Swirler told us all about it in Friday assembly, remember?'

I wrinkled my magnificent forehead, trying to figure out how I'd missed this announcement from our grumpy-fairy dance teacher and School Principal. 'I wasn't in that assembly,' I remembered. 'Madame Swirler sent me out to buy myself some cupcakes.'

'Doesn't sound like her.'

Leotard Girl had a point. Cakey gifts weren't what you'd expect from Madame Swirler.

Leotard Girl was still speaking. 'You must have heard everyone talking about it last night at dinner?'

'Dinner?' I tried to remember. 'Ah. Madame Swirler told me I looked pale and should have a lie down.'

'How can a white unicorn look pale?' Leotard Girl asked.

Miranda gave Leotard Girl a 'look'.

'What?' I asked, worried now. 'Why are you pulling faces, Miranda? Do you think I look pale too?' I pushed my mane away from my face and tested my forehead with the back of my fetlock to see if I had a temperature.

'I still can't see how you haven't heard about this.' Leotard Girl continued, ignoring

Miranda's twitchy facial expressions. It's all everyone's been talking abou—'

Danny bumped Leotard Girl aside with his furry bottom, and put a hoof to my forehead. 'You do feel warm, Louie. Maybe we should head back to the dormitory.'

'I'll be fine,' I said. 'I want to hear more about this dance contest.'

Miranda burst into song:

'♫ We have cake, cake, cake,
In our room, room, room.
If you don't hurry up,
It'll be gone soon, soon, soon ♫.'

Whoa! That changed things.   'Cake? Really? Let's go! Cheerio, Leotard Girl.

Catch you later.'

We ran to the dorm, dragging Miranda's tank along behind us. She reached into her wardrobe for the box labelled 'Emergency Distraction Snacks', and we gobbled up the chocolate cupcakes, discussing our top three cake jokes.

In third place, Frank's favourite: **What does a cat like to eat on his birthday? Cake and mice cream!**

In second place, Danny's choice: **Why couldn't the teddy bear finish his cake?**

Because he was stuffed!

But my joke was the winner! **What's yellow and swings from cake to cake? Tarzipan!**

Funny or what? I love jokes.

It was only as I was falling asleep that I realized I'd forgotten to ask for more information about the dance competition.

Chapter Two

Hip Hop Hysteria

'One . . . two . . . three . . .' Madame Swirler danced across the studio, in front of the floor-to-ceiling mirror, signalling we should move in time with the music.

'. . . Four,' I continued counting, taking another step and knocking Arnie the Unicorn to the ground.

'Owww!' Arnie grabbed his hoof. 'THERE

IS NO FOUR, you horse with a horn. Look what you've done to my foot! It's one, two, three to the right, and then one, two, three to the left. THERE IS NO FOUR. Four is my hoof. Pah! You are clumsier than a buttered donkey on skates.'

The music stopped. Everyone stared.

'Shhh, Arnie,' I hissed. 'People will think we're not BFFs any more.'

'BFFs?' Arnie scoffed. 'You're not my BFF. Unless BFF stands for Baboon with Flat Feet. No wonder everyone's trying to keep the dance competition a secret from you. It would serve you right if they let you enter and you made a big fool of yourse—' Arnie's voice tailed off and his eyes went all shiny. 'Oooh.'

I glanced around the room. No one would look at me. 'Madame Swirler? What's Arnie saying? People aren't really trying to keep this competition a secret from me, are they? No, of course they're not.' I grinned at Arnie. 'You're such a joker.'

'Foolish unicorn,' Madame Swirler muttered, obviously referring to Arnie.

'So you'd like me to be part of the competition?' I asked.

'Um,' she harrumphed, 'Well . . .'

'I'd be marvellous. You know I would. What are the categories?'

'Hip Hop is one,' Arnie said with a snort.

'Oooh, yes. Enter me for the Hip Hop category. Watch this!' I lifted my forelegs until they were level with the floor, twisted my body, and then stopped with a jolt. Checking I had everyone's attention, I locked my forelegs in position for a quick shoulder shrug and waited for applause.

I got none—just a few raised eyebrows and lots of muttering. People were obviously too overwhelmed by my Totally Rad Hip Hop Dance Skillz to waste time cheering. I bent down and shifted my forelegs from right to left, stopping and starting and locking my body in new positions, before finally freezing in place.

I looked up.

Everyone was staring, their mouths making wide 'o's.

I gave a bow.

'Er, what was that?' Miranda asked in a strangled voice.

'I. Was. Doing. The. Robot,' I answered in my best robotic voice. 'It. Is. A. Funky. Hip. Hop. Dance,' I explained.

'Pretty sure it isn't,' Arnie scoffed.

'My dad dances like that,' Leotard Girl said.

'Really?' I smiled. 'Dads are supercool, aren't they?'

'Enough nonsense,' Madame Swirler snapped. 'The Hip Hop slot is already filled.'

A slouchy boy wearing a backwards baseball cap stepped forward, removed his hat and did an impressive head spin.

'Wow! Very good.' I clapped. 'I see why you chose him. Head spins and horns don't really go together. I'd end up screwing myself into the floor. What about the other categories?'

Leotard Girl stepped forward and struck her toe against the floor, making a metallic sound

'Tap?' I guessed, doing a little heel-toe shuffle.

'Yup. But we're disqualified from that category because we can tap without tap shoes,' Arnie told me.

'That's a shame. Well good luck to you, Leotard Girl. I hope you dance as well as your dad.'

'Um. Thank you.'

'I'm entered for the Modern Dance category.' Frank BURPED sheepishly. 'I wanted to tell you, but Madame Swirler said—'

'Zip it, Troll,' Madame Swirler growled. 'So, we have official entrants for four of the five categories—Hip Hop.' She paused for Slouchy Boy to do another head spin. 'Tap.' Leotard Girl beat out a rhythm on the gym floors. 'Modern dance.' Frank gave a reluctant twirl. 'And disco.' A small girl in a bright–yellow silk dress and lime–green leggings raised her arms in the air and shook her hips at me.

'Hello and congratulations.' I beamed at them all. 'What about the fifth category?'

'Ballet. We're discussing it with the judges as we'd like to enter someone with four legs instead of two.'

I looked at my front legs. I looked at my back legs. I counted them. A huge smile broke out across my face.

'And that someone would be Arnie,' Madame Swirler added.

I felt as though a large postal sack full of fan mail and fluffy toys addressed to someone else had fallen from the ceiling and crushed me.

'I'm sure he'll be wonderful,' I said, squishing my disappointment. Arnie was my friend. I was happy for him.

It would have been nice to get a chance to audition though. To show them what they were missing, I leapt from the floor and did the splits in the air. It was magnificent until I hit the whirling legs of Hip Hop Slouchy Boy, mid head spin.

Knocked sideways, I flew across the room in the direction of Miranda's tank. Miranda squealed and pressed herself against the glass walls as I landed with an almighty splash.

I was worried she wouldn't have enough water left to swim in, given the amount that had gone in my nose and mouth. Perhaps this was how it felt to be a shark.

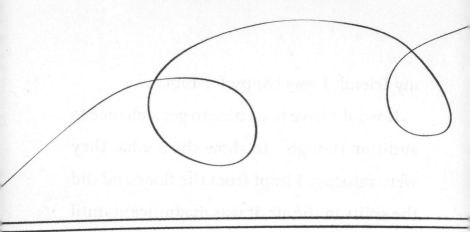

Probably not.

Probably closer to how it felt to be a drowning unicorn.

Frank thrust his hand in the water and yanked me out, flopping me over the top of the tank. 'Lesson's over,' he said, wheeling me and Miranda to drama class.

'I'm sure that impressed them,' I spluttered, giving the watching crowd a wave.

The only person who waved back was Arnie, who mouthed, 'I'll fix you, Louie the Unicorn.'

Awww. Arnie wanted to fix things. What a lovely friend he was.

Chapter Three

Name Swapping

Madame Swirler announced that the judges had happily accepted a unicorn in the ballet category the minute they saw video footage of Arnie doing five Double Tours in the air. Their only condition was he had to wear tights and a leotard like the other competitors.

I don't know why everyone found Arnie's Double Tour jumps so impressive. Anyone could jump and twirl round in the sky like that . . . as long as no one minded if they got a bit dizzy afterwards and fell down the stairs, causing hundreds of dollars of damage to Madame Swirler's Royal Doulton figurine collection.

I worked hard gluing the first one back together. Then Danny peered through his glasses and pointed out I'd stuck the top of a ballerina figurine to the bottom halves of a pair of ballroom dancers.

Oops!

You'd think I'd get credit for trying. Didn't.

It wasn't as if *I* escaped unharmed either. The pointed toe of the ballet–dancing figurine—now glued below the smiling faces of the ballroom dancers—left a nasty bruise on my thigh.

But it didn't matter. Arnie was accepted and all the competition places were full. No use crying over spilt milk—or over Royal Doulton ballerinas with too many legs.

But maybe I'd spoken too soon.

Madame Swirler had put Arnie in charge of sending the entry forms and the application process must have confused him, because two days later a list of competitors was pinned to the wall and it looked like this:

'Hmmm.' I scratched my horn. I

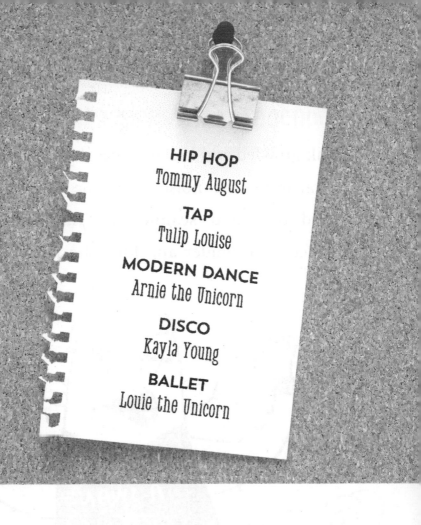

HIP HOP
Tommy August

TAP
Tulip Louise

MODERN DANCE
Arnie the Unicorn

DISCO
Kayla Young

BALLET
Louie the Unicorn

LOVED the list, but I knew it wasn't supposed to look like this. I glanced up anxiously as Frank came round the corner. He wasn't going to like it.

'ROOOOOOAAAAARRRRRRRRRRRRR!'

Frank growled and kicked a nearby bin.

Drawn by the noise, Madame Swirler darted over and scanned the list. She growled even louder and kicked a nearby Frank.

Fortunately, Frank was too furious (and furry) to feel it. 'What is Arnie playing at?' he bellowed. 'This is a disaster!'

'I know!' Madame Swirler was more upset than I'd ever seen her. 'This was our chance to win the ballet category. Arnie could have made everyone forget the last five years of bad performances and shown them that the New York School for Performing Arts *can* teach great ballet.' With an angry flap of her wings, she declared, 'I'm calling the judges this instant. I will not let a mistake with the forms ruin things for everyone.'

'Well . . . not quite everyone,' I said quietly.

'Arnie did this on purpose,' Frank bellowed, still roaring at full volume as

Madame Swirler stomped off.

'You think so?' Was Frank right? Had Arnie done it deliberately? Changed things so I could be part of the competition? Maybe he really *was* my BFF.

'I *know* so,' Frank pulled a napkin from his baby-shaped lunchbox and dabbed his eyes. He was quieter now. 'I know you think Arnie's wonderful, Louie. But he's not.'

Danny and Miranda joined us. They gasped at the list and Miranda patted Frank sympathetically before bursting into song:

'♩ Arnie is a fool,
Who thinks he's super cool,
But everyone at school,
knows Arnie is a mule (with a horn)♩.'

'Miranda!' I shook my head. 'That's a terrible thing to sing. Look at everything Arnie's done for me.'

'For you? What are you talking about, Louie? Have you been chomping on out-of-date doughnuts again?'

'No! Although those custard ones were in my cupboard for a week . . . Anyway, the point is, Arnie only did this because he realized how good I'd be in the ballet competition.'

Miranda coughed and spluttered. She must be poorly. Maybe we should change the water in her tank.

To make her feel better, I showed her a couple of my best ballet moves.

Danny giggled.

'Oi!' I protested.

'You mean you weren't trying to be funny?' Danny turned to Frank and Miranda. 'He wasn't trying to be funny?'

They shook their heads.

I rolled my eyes. 'Stop teasing. I know my moves are spectacular. I showed Arnie earlier and he said they were out of this world. Or maybe he said they were like something from another planet? Either way, he was very positive. Now, shhh.'

Chapter Four

Pot Plant Confessions

I trotted into the corridor that led to the dormitories, in search of my ballet shoes. A large pot plant blocked my view, so I heard Miranda and Danny before I saw them.

'We have to save him,' Miranda was saying.

'I know,' Danny agreed. 'The competition will be humiliating. He's a lovely unicorn and I don't want to see him upset.'

'Agreed. Now, hush! Louie will be here soon.'

'Too late, roomies.' I jumped out from behind the indoor bush. 'Already here.'

They both flushed red and started fidgeting.

'Don't worry,' I reassured them. 'I completely understand what you were saying.'

'You do?'

'You're worried about Arnie embarrassing himself in the Modern Dance category.'

'We are?' Miranda peered through the glass of her tank at Danny.

'Sure. Let's say we're talking about Arnie.' Danny pushed his glasses up his nose. 'Now, on a completely different subject, Louie, have you thought about what'll happen if you take part in this competition? It means EVERYTHING to Madame Swirler. Our school hasn't finished in the top three of the ballet category for five years. If we fail again, we won't be allowed to enter next year. The school's reputation depends on this. One bad performance and—'

'Bad performance?' I laughed. 'How can I give a bad performance? I am Louie the Unicorn.'

'Yeah, and they're expecting Arnie the Unicorn with his five Double Tours,' Danny pointed out.

'That's just spinning. Anyone can spin. I can spin plates. I can spin doughnuts. All I have to do is spin ME.'

I gave Danny and Miranda a big grin and leapt into my first Double Tour, whirling and spinning 360 degrees, enjoying the whip of my mane against my face.

As I landed the first jump and leapt up into the second, I saw Madame Swirler at the far end of the corridor.

This was the perfect opportunity to impress her and it was going well. Crashing into the pot plant just added to the excitement, and the group of students who ducked to avoid

having their heads knocked off by a flying curtain rail simply made my jumps look even higher.

By the fourth jump I was feeling a little dizzy and by the fifth there were stars in front of my eyes. Because of a slight miscalculation, I jumped more sideways than upwards on the final leap and landed on a cleaning trolley.

I clung to the trolley as it shot down the corridor. Everyone leapt out of the way until I eventually ground to a halt in front of Madame Swirler.

OK, things hadn't gone exactly to plan. But Dad always told me being a Dashing Unicorn is all about presentation.

'Ta da,' I announced with my best unicorn grin.

Madame Swirler grabbed the handle of the cleaning trolley and wheeled me away from everyone, muttering under her breath. 'You are a truly foolish unicorn. And yet it seems that if the New York School for Performing Arts is to avoid the worst humiliation in its history, I will have to personally tutor you in ballet.'

I gazed at Madame Swirler in shock and delight. This was the ultimate honour. Madame Swirler never did one-to-one tutoring. There were rumours the school governors had forbidden it after she gave lessons in the quickstep to an army major and he ran away in tears after the first session.

But I was safe. Madame Swirler LOVED me. I knew she did. Just like I knew it was an accident when she kicked my cleaning trolley into the wall and squished my leg.

Chapter Five

Scary Moves and Scary Movies

'**R**ight, you daft creature.' Madame Swirler pushed me and my cleaning trolley into her office. 'Sit up and pay attention. I'll take you through the ballet routine I planned with Arnie and then we'll work out how to get you in shape.'

'Can I begin by saying how pleased I am that you have faith in me to do this,

Madame Swirler?'

'Pah! I have no faith in you at all, idiot unicorn. I've been on the phone for two hours trying to get the judges to admit they made a mistake with the forms so we can change things back to the way they should be. But they are being very unreasonable and insist they have to take the names that were given. I blame Rudolph Trollyev.'

'The famous ballet dancer?' I asked. 'I didn't know he was one of the judges? I hear he's wonderful.'

Madame Swirler's face went twisty and turny, and a strange noise came from her throat. If she'd been Frank I'd have thought she was about to do a massive burp, but Madame Swirler was a fairy. Fairies don't do that kind of thing.

'Rudolph Trollyev is not a judge. He's a coach and he is NOT remotely wonderful. In fact, he may be the only person in the universe who annoys me more than you do.'

I thought about that for a while. 'So, you're saying you like me more than one of the world's most successful male ballet dancers? COOL!'

Madame Swirler made the same roary, burpy sound and reached for my neck.

I edged further back on the trolley, making it wobble. 'So, shall we go through that routine you were talking about?'

'Hmmmph. Probably should.' Madame Swirler lost the murderous expression and pressed a few buttons on her computer. 'I filmed Arnie going through some of the moves last week. See what you think.'

We watched a ballet sequence that looked more like a gymnastic routine. My main thought was 'Eeek!'

Madame Swirler paused it for a moment. 'This is where you do the five Double Tours.'

'About that,' I said slowly. 'I was wondering if perhaps we could make it *four* Double Tours. Things didn't go so well on the fifth one.' I rolled over on the cleaning trolley and rubbed my leg where it had been bashed against the wall. My hand came away covered in red goo.

'Blood.' I collapsed back onto the trolley and howled. 'I'm covered in blood. Oh my!'

Madame Swirler glared at me. 'It's

ketchup, you fool. You're covered in ketchup. That's what you get for rolling around on trolleys used to pick up rubbish.'

'Ketchup? Really? Oooh, yes, look! Mustard too.' I licked my hoof. 'Mmmmm.' Fuelled by sugary hot dog accompaniments I felt confident again. 'So, five Double Tours? No problem. That's the hardest bit, right?'

'Wrong.' Madame Swirler said. 'We have to win this tournament. The school's reputation depends on it and we need to show that idiot Rudolph Trollyev who's the best. Since you have no grace, we have to go for difficulty points. So you'll be doing a move called the Leaping Champion.'

'The what?'

'A new move I've invented. Almost impossible to perform.'

'Er. Good?' I said, as this seemed to be expected.

'Watch.' Madame Swirler turned off the Arnie-Does-Ballet film and put on an

animation showing a stick figure springing up from the left leg and extending all four legs out, like a star jump, then leaping higher still into a forward somersault.

'Um? This seems to require me to defeat the laws of gravity,' I pointed out, timidly.

'WE CANNOT LET THAT TROLLEY EV MAN WIN!'

'Which makes it a really great jump,' I continued, mainly because Madame Swirler looked ready to punch something and I was the nearest something. 'Why is it animated rather than in film like everything else?'

'Because no one has ever achieved this leap in real life. Yet.'

Yikes. 'And you want me to try it? In here?'

Madame Swirler looked around her office, taking in her photo frames, trophies and treasured ornaments. 'No. Let's go to the dance studio. And Louie . . .?'

'Yes, Miss Swirler?'

'Get down off that trolley.'

Chapter Six

Battered Unicorn

Some people have asked me why unicorns don't get bruises. Those people are silly. Unicorns DO get bruises. You just can't see them under our handsome fur coats. I know this because I AM COVERED IN BRUISES. My whole body hurts.

'Poor ballet dancers,' I said to Frank, who'd carried bruised-yet-still-dashing me all the way to the school theatre, where he continued to practise his Modern Dance routine every day, despite Arnie taking his place in the competition. 'They must be in constant pain.'

'Don't take this the wrong way,' Frank said. 'But I don't think other ballet dancers bump into quite as many things as you do.'

Hmmm. That might be true. I looked around the theatre. There were several holes in the walls, a man was hammering behind the curtain to cover the large hole in the stage, and no one had decided what to do with the remains of the piano I'd landed on yesterday. The place was empty too. After the first three horn-related injuries, everyone had stopped visiting the theatre if they knew I was practising. Everyone except Frank. And, of course, Madame Swirler.

Madame Swirler had been a talented ballet dancer when she was young and was now a brilliant (if slightly scary) teacher. I was a huge fan and every so often I got the urge to grab her and give her a big unicorn cuddle. Of course, she pretended she hated it. To be honest, she was good at pretending. The marks from her punches stood out, even among all the ballet bruises.

There she was, looking wonderfully glarey. I couldn't help it. I moved towards her, forelegs outstretched. 'Huggies?'

'NO HUGGIES!' She glared at me. 'We are running out of time and you still haven't

done a successful Leaping Champion jump.
Perhaps it would help if we found you a
softer landing place to practise on. Water
might be the answer. Let's go to Central
Park Lake.'

Chapter Seven

To the Lake

'Central Park Lake?' I stared at Madame Swirler in alarm. 'But I can't swim.'

'Good,' she said. 'More incentive to land the jump well.'

'Haha?' I mumbled uncertainly.

Frank stopped rehearsing, gave me a reassuring pat and told me he was going upstairs to talk to Danny and Miranda.

As a result, when I returned to the dorm Miranda handed me a pair of armbands.

'Um, thank you,' I said. 'But you're a mermaid. Why do you have armbands?'

Miranda blushed. 'I had a boyfriend who couldn't swim.'

I didn't join in the teasing. It would have been rude when she'd given me inflatable swimming aids and offered to come with me to Central Park. Even with the armbands, I was still nervous. Miranda saw me trembling and ordered Danny and Frank to come along too.

I gazed at the lake in alarm. It looked dark, deep and not at all inviting.

My legs shook, but my father's voice echoed through my mind: 'Unicorns are never afraid. Unicorns can do anything. It's all about belief. If you do anything as a unicorn, it must be done with Dash and Derring-Do.'

I would NOT let this Leaping Champion jump defeat me. If launching myself into a murky lake was what it took to make this leap, then I would launch myself into the lake.

Oh yes! In this battle of Unicorn versus Lake, I, Louie the Unicorn, would emerge the victor.

I ran towards the lake at top speed,

holding my nose to keep the water out. I was magnificent, just as my father had predicted. Unfortunately, I forgot to jump, but this was just a first attempt—I couldn't be expected to get everything right first time.

I skimmed across the surface of the lake, using my hooves like one of those water skiers you see on television, leaning backwards to wave a foreleg at the onlookers who'd gathered. If only I'd brought my fiery torches. I could have juggled to impress them further.

Uh oh! Something was wrong. I'd run out of ooomph. The water was rising: above my hooves, above my knees. Oh, no! My dashing mane! Water lapped at my belly and the armbands made me all lopsided. I tried to regain my speed, kicking out at the water, legs whirring like overactive hamsters in plastic balls—hamsters who

didn't want to get their ears wet. But it was no good. Unicorns are heavier than water.

'Louie?' Madame Swirler snapped. 'What on Earth are you doing?'

'Conquering my fear of the lake,' I spluttered, spitting out a small fish. 'Sort of.'

'Well, do it over here where it's shallower, numpty. There's still enough water to soften the landing from the jump. Louie, stop all that splashing! This instant!'

'Will do, Madame Swirler! Just let me finish siiiiiiiiiiiiinking.' Gurgle. 'Water in my nose! Eek! Fish in my ear! FISH IN MY EAR!'

I felt a tugging sensation and was plucked from the murky water by a rower, who hooked his oar through my 'I ♡ NY' T-shirt and deposited me at the side of the lake. I tried to thank him, but water came out instead of words. A lot of coughing later, I finally managed a spluttery 'thanks',

but by then he was gone.

Feeling bedraggled, with my usually resplendent tail tucked, damply, between my legs, I slunk across to join Madame Swirler.

She shook her head at me, but not unkindly. 'Louie, you are the most infuriating creature I know, but if self-belief won medals, you'd be wearing your weight in gold.'

'Good thing I'm not,' I said, thinking about it. 'The weight would have dragged me to the bottom of the lake.'

'Enough silliness.' Madame Swirler rolled up her sleeves. 'Rudolph Trollyev would not wait for a unicorn in armbands to dry off. DO THE JUMP!'

For what felt like the millionth time, I did my run-up and launched myself into the air. Madame Swirler was right about the water. There was definitely less bruising, which was a relief as I didn't have many bruise-free areas left. In fact, it was all going very well indeed, until the Central Park boatman approached.

'NO MORE SPLASHING!' he bellowed. 'I'm tired, I'm wet, and I've had enough. I've spent the last half an hour apologizing to the people you've drenched with water. ENOUGH IS ENOUGH. Time to go home.'

Frank, Danny and Miranda all BOO-ed him from their dry, grassy spot beneath a nearby tree, but part of me sympathized with him. I knew what it felt like to be very, very wet.

Madame Swirler stepped forward and got all grumpy-fairy in his face. 'Leave this unicorn alone,' she snapped. 'He's trying his best.'

Wow! Madame Swirler was sticking up for me! I took a step backward in surprise.

'*This unicorn* has been terrorizing the Central Park boating community,' the boatman snapped back.

'Hardly!' Madame Swirler's wings twitched in rage. 'Louie has done an excellent job today, despite being scared and useless.'

I considered being offended by 'useless', but decided to focus on how nice it felt to be defended by Madame Swirler. HUGS! I touched my heart with my hoof and took another backwards step.

'Look at him!' Madame Swirler pointed at me and I gave an awkward wave in response. 'He might look like a soggy mess, but Louie is a unicorn with the heart of a lion. We'll make a ballet dancer of him yet!'

She liked my heart! She thought I'd make a wonderful ballet dancer! Overwhelmed,

I stepped back again. But this time I ran out of grass.

I hit the lake and suddenly it was all

SPLASH! GLUG! `HELP!'

Water flew over the nearest rowers, and the wave I'd accidentally created overturned their boat, sending the three teenagers inside hurtling into the water.

`GRRRRR!' The boatman leapt into the lake to help.

'It's OK,' I called to reassure him as my hoof touched ground. 'I'm fine.'

He growled more loudly, and after helping the teenagers to shore, he pulled a fish from his armpit and started half-wading, half-swimming towards me, muttering threats about de-horning unicorns.

Yikes! Run away!

Without thinking, I took up the position for the Leaping Champion as the boatman approached. Testing the ground and trying not to think too hard about the squelchy thing beneath my feet, I sprang from the lake into an energetic star jump, with enough power and energy to launch a perfectly executed forward somersault.

I DID IT!

I couldn't believe it.

I DID IT!

I got a standing ovation from my friends beneath the tree.

Even Madame Swirler clapped. 'Oh, Louie, that was a perfect Leaping Champion!' She grabbed my foreleg as the boatman reached for my tail. 'We'll celebrate later. Right now, we should probably run.'

As we raced through the park, with Danny and Frank lolloping along behind us, carrying Miranda and her tank, I could have sworn I heard Madame Swirler giggle. But that was even more impossible than completing a Leaping Champion jump.

Chapter Eight

Fire-breathing Dragons

Full of enthusiasm (and accidentally-swallowed lake water) after my one and only successful Leaping Champion jump, I was ready for our final week of rehearsals.

I couldn't wait to meet my fellow contestants from the competing schools. Arnie kept joking about 'taking them down' and 'wiping them out'. But I was sure we'd all get along marvellously.

The person I was most excited about meeting was one of the dancers in my category—Desdemona the Dragon. Rumour had it Desdemona had been asked to join the Bolshoi Ballet, the Paris Opera Ballet, the Stuttgart Ballet AND the New York City Ballet, all before her fourteenth birthday. Apparently her parents said she had to finish school first because it was important for dragons to have good qualifications to fall back on.

Still, I bet she'd never Leaping Champion-ed out of a lake with an angry boatman in hot pursuit. So, while I was curious to meet this legend of the ballet world, I was confident the trophy was mine.

But first I had to do the Leaping Champion

on an actual stage, without water. I wanted to live up to Madame Swirler's expectations because I could see how hard she was working and how important this was to her. So, ignoring the pain and the bumps and the tumbles over pianos, into mirrors, and out of windows, I continued to bounce and leap and jump and fly through the air on her command.

I was SO close to achieving the jump again. But, as Madame Swirler kept reminding me, close wasn't good enough. I just couldn't repeat my Central Park Lake performance, however hard I tried.

Four days before the final contest, there was a kerfuffle at the back of the theatre where we were rehearsing. It was hard to see clearly as the stage lights were shining in my eyes, but I heard Frank, Danny and Miranda murmur 'Rudolph Trollyev' in hushed tones.

I moved out of the light for a better view and immediately recognized the tall, dark visitor from a hundred magazine covers that had featured his distinguished face and muscly dancer's body.

Madame Swirler waved for me to continue practising, but it was hard with Rudolph Trollyev sitting out there in the audience, scribbling notes and making comments. Comments that weren't as nice as you'd expect if you'd read his marvellous magazine interviews.

Madame Swirler's face grew increasingly purple with every minute.

After I failed my seventeenth attempt, Rudolph Trollyev tossed his head and rose to leave, declaring loudly: 'This is no champion. The creature is lumpen like dough, and lacks the energy to jump high. He has no chance against my Desdemona.'

Madame Swirler stomped after him as he exited the theatre. I'd never seen her so scowly. Not even that time we sang the song about her being really, really old on her last birthday.

Maybe I should be scowly too? I had been called 'lumpen like dough'. But scowly seemed a waste of time and I liked dough—dough made cookies. Instead, I raced after them, and as I barged through the door I saw Rudolph Trollyev give Madame Swirler a strange, toothy smile. 'If it isn't my little Sugar Plump Fairy.'

'It's Plum,' I told him. He obviously didn't speak English well. 'P-L-U-M. What you said was—'

'Thank you, Louie,' Madame Swirler snapped. 'He knows what he said.'

'But he called you—'

'Stop speaking, Louie,' Arnie appeared at my elbow. 'You really don't have a clue, do you?'

'A clue? Are we playing a game?' I turned to Arnie in excitement. 'I like games.'

Rudolph Trollyev sneered at Madame Swirler. 'You entered these foolish creatures into the dance competition?'

'Yes, she did,' I answered eagerly. 'And we're thrilled.'

Arnie kicked me.

'I know a joke about unicorns,' Mr Trollyev said.

'Oh goody,' I jumped up and down. 'I love jokes.'

'Why don't unicorns make good dancers?'

'This doesn't sound like a joke I'll like,' Arnie harrumphed.

Rudolph Trollyev ignored him and roared the punchline. 'Because they have two left feet! Haha! Two left feet!'

I agreed with Arnie. I didn't like the joke either. But I had no time to respond because Arnie grabbed me in a tight hug. This wasn't like him. Awww, the joke must have made him sad. I leaned in to cuddle him back and almost fell over my feet when Arnie began twirling me round. Next thing I knew, I was flying towards Rudolph Trollyev at top speed.

'Whoa!' I panicked and tried to regain my balance, but it was too late. I shut my eyes and prepared for impact.

OOOF!

'SORRY! SORRY! SORRY!' I squeaked, trying to pull my horn out of Mr Trollyev's perfectly groomed beard. 'Accident!'

While I was unhooking myself, I heard a strange hissing sound and a flame shot past my ear. There was a strong smell of burning unicorn hair. I patted my mane in panic but it was fine.

'Noooooo!' Arnie whinnied in horror, staring at his previously perfect but now slightly singed tail. 'How dare you . . . Oh.'

He swallowed his protests as a shimmering green dragon

AAAAAAAHH!!

81

stepped out from the shadows, fire still splurting from her nostrils.

I inched towards her carefully and held out my hoof, 'You must be Desdemona. I've been looking forward to meeting you. I've heard such amazing things.'

Desdemona looked through me as if I didn't exist. Maybe unicorns were invisible to dragons? I tried a little wave instead.

She snorted out another flame in response. I wasn't invisible then! When the blaze died down I tried again. 'Um. Lovely to meet you, Desdemona. I'm Louie the Unicorn.'

She stared down her smoking nose at me. 'You will not speak to me.'

'I won't?'

'Absolutely not. You are the enemy.'

'I'm *not* the enemy. I'm the good guy. Tell her, Arnie.'

Arnie just grunted.

'You are *my* enemy,' the dragon insisted. 'Competing ballet dancers can never be friends.'

'They can't?' I sighed. 'Well, that's a shame because you seem lovely.'

Desdemona blinked. 'I do?'

'Oh yes. All green and shiny and fiery. Very cool.'

Her huge round dragon eyes widened and she opened her mouth to speak, but at that moment, Rudolph Trollyev muscled his way forward, rubbing his beard to display a unicorn-horn-shaped hole. I hung my head in shame.

Desdemona shot out another flame, close to my head. 'You, unicorn, are not cool. Not cool at all. How dare you poke Mr Trollyev with your pointy spike? How dare you

challenge me in this ballet competition? You are nothing, puny creature. I will crush you.'

She shot another flame towards Arnie. 'I will crush you all. You are insignificant mythical creatures and your school is an insignificant nothing school. Soon people will laugh at the sound of its name. The only school worth attending is the East Coast School of Dance. So there! Pah!' And with a huge puff of smoke, she stormed out of the theatre.

Silence.

'Well, that didn't go so badly,' I said. 'Nothing important caught fire. We still have all our limbs.'

'Shut up, Louie,' Arnie whinnied. 'I

thought it'd be fun to watch you mess up, but this is a disaster. The whole school's reputation is at stake and my beautiful tail has been toasted. We can't let that dragon-diva defeat us. I hate to say it, but I want you to win this category, Louie.'

'"Watch me mess up"? Arnie have you bumped your head during your Modern Dance routine?' I asked in concern. 'And why would you *hate* to say you wanted me to win? Everyone knows you're my biggest supporter.'

There were snorts from the other students. Was everyone coming down with a cold? Maybe fire-breathing dragons carried germs?

Madame Swirler stepped forward. 'For once in your life, foolish unicorn, you need to join the real world. I refuse to let Rudolph Trollyev and his pet dragon destroy our reputation. We will make you the best ballet dancer this theatre has ever seen, WHATEVER IT TAKES.'

I shivered.

Must be those dragon germs.

Chapter Nine

Ankle Grabbing

'**You** must defeat that bully, Rudolph Trollyev,' Madame Swirler growled.

'You must defeat that diva, Desdemona the Dragon,' Arnie roared.

'You must do your best!' Miranda, Danny and Frank said. 'That's all that matters.'

My friends were lovely, but on this occasion I wasn't convinced they were right. I WAS doing my best. I was doing better than my best! But Madame Swirler kept on yelling and Arnie kept frowning.

'I should never have changed the entry forms,' Arnie muttered as the school nurse draped another ice pack over my leg. 'This is a nightmare.'

'You're admitting you *did* do it on purpose?' A warm glow pierced the chill of the ice pack. 'You fiddled things so I could join the competition! I knew it!' I sighed happily. 'All because you could see how much I wanted to be part of it.'

'All because I wanted everyone to see how useless you are,' Arnie muttered.

'Huh?' I stuck a hoof in my ear and

jiggled it about. My ears must be full of wax. Or maybe I still had a fish in there.

Arnie tossed his mane. 'I just hadn't realized the whole school's reputation was at stake. Don't make us all look like losers.'

I didn't intend to make anyone look like a loser. I could do this. I'd done it once; I must be able to do it again. Madame Swirler seemed to be thinking along the same lines.

'What was different in the lake, Louie? Why could you do it there?'

'I was scared of the angry boatman,' I said. 'And I trod on something that might have been a frog, which gave me extra bounce.'

'I could scare you,' Frank the Troll offered, taking a deep breath.

'ROOOOAAAAAAAAAAAAAARRR!'

Lots of people squealed, one fainted, and several had to go to the bathroom. Frank did good scary, until he ruined it with a

loud, 'BURP!' at the end.

I shook my head. 'You can't scare me, Frank. I know how kind you are. Your roaring won't make me jump. Sorry.'

Danny stepped forward. 'It's late at night,' he said in a strangely deep voice. 'You go up to our dorm room alone, knowing we're all down here rehearsing. The room is dark. You reach out to turn on the light switch . . . but a hand is already there.'

'Ewww, Danny,' I protested. 'Why so creepy?'

'I'm trying to scare you,' he said. 'To make you jump.'

'Er. Thanks?'

As I tried to explain the different kinds of scary, something grabbed my ankles and launched me into the air.

I didn't panic. I'd practised the Leaping Champion jump until it was part of my muscle memory, so as I flew through the air I automatically launched into the jump . . . AND I NAILED IT!

Leapingchampiontastic!

Everyone cheered. I looked to see what had aided my launch, but all I could see was Arnie blowing on his front hooves and whistling innocently.

'Arnie?' I asked him. 'Did you see who sent me flying?'

'Me? Why would *I* have seen anything?

It's not like *I* would have helped you or anything. Stop going on about it and just be glad you finally made the jump. Maybe this competition won't end in utter humiliation for everyone.'

'But I didn't do it. Somebody flung me in the air.'

'Shhh!' Arnie hissed. 'All you have to do is repeat what just happened in the competition.' Arnie flexed his muscles and made a strange throwing movement. 'And, somehow, I think you will.'

Chapter Ten

Pond Scum

The day of the competition dawned. I was in a happy place. Madame Swirler was almost pleased with me, Arnie said he wanted to stay by my side during my whole routine (awww), and when I practised in the dressing room I only knocked one glass and two hairbrushes off the table.

'You're sure you want to do this?' Frank checked as

Danny picked up the brushes.

I nodded enthusiastically.

'In that case . . .' He reached behind his back and pulled out a cake in the shape of a unicorn doing a star jump. He, Danny and Miranda yelled, 'GOOD LUCK, LOUIE!'

I clapped in delight. 'Frank, this is so nice of you. Especially considering . . .' I stopped clapping as I remembered Frank would still be in the competition if I wasn't.

'It's not your fault, Louie.' Frank cut me a huge slice of cake, looked at it and then stuffed it into his mouth. 'Sorry!' he mumbled. 'Troll urges! What was I saying? Oh yes. This is Arnie's doing.'

I still felt guilty. Especially when Miranda handed me a gift-wrapped box. However, the guilt wore off when I opened it and found it contained a leotard and a pair of tights. I tried not to look ungrateful, but I already had those things and didn't like them very much. Tights and leotards do not make unicorns look dashing.

'They're flame-resistant,' Miranda beamed. 'Put them on. You're competing with a fire-breathing dragon. We don't want you to get burnt.'

'Don't be silly,' I said, but I put the fire-resistant outfit on just in case. 'I'm sure Desdemona the Dragon is a pussy cat underneath.'

'A fire-breathing pussycat,' Miranda muttered as we headed down to the competition.

At first glance, this could have been any gathering of humans and mythical creatures. But if you looked closely you could tell there was something unusual going on. Everyone was stretching and subtly eyeing up the competition.

Meanwhile, on the other side of the room, Rudolph Trollyev was shouting at his star pupil. Desdemona looked even more uncomfortable in her ballet tights and leotard than I felt. Perhaps because, being a girl-dragon, she also had to wear a tutu. I saw a few scorch marks on it.

'Listen to the music!' Rudolph Trollyev yelled.

Desdemona's moves were perfect but she stared at Mr Trollyev with wide, nervous eyes.

'It is not enough to be perfect. You must make these other competitors look like pond scum who have climbed out of the water, onto the road, and then been run over.'

'Thanks,' said another girl in our category.

Everyone was tense. We knew we had to grab the judge's attention quickly if we wanted to win. And we all wanted to win.

Chapter Eleven

The Big Contest

Backstage was dark and quiet. Nerves swallowed people's voices. But then the curtains opened and light filled the room. There were eight competitors in my category. Desdemona was drawn last, with me just before her. So, six ballet performances before mine. I pretended to practise but I was really watching them. They were all very lovely—no run-over pond scum there. But no Leaping Champions either.

My name was called. I pulled up my tights, adjusted my tail in my leotard, and prepared for my victory routine.

As I swirled on stage, several hundred sets of eyes watched me closely. Yikes! Madame Swirler had said that if I felt scared I should imagine everyone in the audience wearing only their underwear. But that was even scarier. Perhaps my imagination was too good because some had very strange imaginary pants on. Especially that guy in the second row.

I shook my head and tried to get into a ballet mindset. Focus! Leap, star jump, somersault, landing, applause, bow, trophy.

I spotted Arnie at the side of the stage, flexing his muscles. What support! I felt a rush of confidence. Madame Swirler and Arnie believed in me. This was my time to shine.

I'd practised so often that the first part of the routine came easily and I relaxed into the positions. I hadn't knocked anything over or created any holes so far. This was a triumph. I took a deep breath as the time came for the Double Tours.

One . . . no one hurt.

Two . . . no one hurt.

Three . . . no one hurt.

Four . . . no one hurt.

Five . . . uh oh, kicked a water bottle into the crowd and whacked a Hip Hopper on the nose.

I looked at Madame Swirler in alarm but she gave me our agreed signal for 'No ambulance required. Carry on.' So I launched into my Grand Jeté. Guaranteed points.

Now it was time for the Leaping Champion. I ran through it in my brain. Spring from left, extend all legs like a star, spring higher into that perfect forward somersault. Mentally prepared, I moved with all the grace within me (not much, according to Madame Swirler, but she did like to tease) and began my run up.

As I bounded along the side of the stage I felt that same touch on my ankle and, without warning, I found myself flying through the air. Whoa! What was happening? The only person anywhere near me was Arnie. Surely he couldn't have . . .?

But it seemed he had. When I looked at him questioningly, he nodded impatiently and hissed, 'Whatever. Just get on with it, stupid.'

No! This was wrong! Despite my body automatically moving into position for the Leaping Champion I bought myself down to the ground, ignoring Arnie's whinny of protest as I began a second run-up.

Rudolph Trollyev sprang to his feet and bounded towards the stage, roaring, 'Stop! Cheats! Rule-breaking unicorns!'

Terrified of what he'd do when he reached me, I leapt into the air, visualizing myself jumping away from him and towards the safety of a giant cupcake. I flew across the stage, picturing myself as a handsome winged pegacorn, and completed the star jump and somersault with ease.

The crowd roared their approval as I finished my routine and bowed. Madame Swirler punched the air in the strongest display of non-anger-related emotion I'd ever seen from her.

I liked the air-punching and the applause but my head felt fuzzy as I left the stage. What had just happened? Rudolph Trollyev was still storming towards me. I, in turn, stormed towards Arnie. How dare he try to make me cheat? That was not UNICORN behaviour!

At that moment, Desdemona's backing music started. I sat back down. Rude to interrupt someone else's performance. Rudolph Trollyev did the same.

Desdemona looked slightly awkward as she stepped into the spotlight, tugging her tutu, but when she began to dance all traces of self-consciousness vanished. She shimmered, she shone, she was on fire— literally at some points. Luckily some of her fellow students were carrying fire extinguishers.

It was a very difficult routine. Similar to my own. In fact, it was REALLY similar to my own. The only difference was Desdemona did one more repetition of every difficult move.

After the sixth Double Tour, Madame Swirler's forehead creased. Following the two Grand Jetés, Madame Swirler threw a pen at Rudolph Trollyev. And when Desdemona launched into her second Leaping Champion, Madame Swirler's voice echoed around the room.

'You can't pretend that was accidental. I INVENTED that move. It didn't even exist before I came up with it.'

I remembered all the notes Mr Trollyev had taken during my practice session. My horn tingled with righteous indignation.

The kerfuffle between the two coaches had caught Desdemona's attention.

'Tell me it's not true,' she begged Rudolph Trollyev as she landed her final jump to a standing ovation, and climbed off the stage. 'Tell me you didn't steal their jump.'

'It's all your fault,' he scowled. 'You made it look too similar.'

A fat tear rolled down Desdemona's green-scaled face, turning to steam as it reached her fire-breathing nostrils.

'Of course the jump looked similar,' Madame Swirler shrieked. 'You copied it!'

'Copied?' Rudolph Trollyev's scoffed. 'Pah! You dare accuse me, Sugar Plump Fairy? You, with your cheating unicorns? You are just angry because you have been in love with me for years and I do not return your feelings.'

Madame Swirler seemed to shrink. Desdemona was still sobbing. Everyone was sad. Unacceptable! As a Dashing Unicorn it was my job to fix this.

I turned to the judges. 'I think that, despite excellent competition . . .' I paused to give everyone time to realize *I* was the excellent competition, 'Desdemona was the best ballerina today.' My voice grew stronger as I remembered Arnie's efforts to help me cheat. I didn't want to win with that on my conscience. 'She had nothing to do with stealing the routine. Desdemona is the worthy winner.'

A chant of 'Des-de-mon-a' echoed through the room. I was happy to hear a few 'Lou-ies' too and waved at Frank, Danny and Miranda.

The judges handed Desdemona the huge

BALLET CHAMPION trophy and more tears leaked from her eyes.

'Happy tears,' she reassured me, blowing her nose on her tutu, which burst into flames. 'Perhaps we don't *have* to be enemies, unicorn.'

I smiled at my new friend and then turned to glare at Rudolph Trollyev. 'You, sir, are not as nice as you should be.'

Danny, Frank and Miranda gasped.

'But . . . But . . . you think everyone's nice!' Miranda spluttered.

'Not this man. He upset Desdemona and embarrassed my favourite teacher. I must defend the honour of these beautiful maidens.'

Desdemona blushed. Madame Swirler

glared at everyone who giggled at the 'beautiful maidens' description.

'Louie the Unicorn!' one of the judges walked across to join us. 'For your unselfishness and your dazzling performance, we'd like to award you second place and a Highly Commended Certificate.'

Wow! Who needed a trophy? You couldn't frame a trophy. This certificate could hang on the wall of my dormitory, in pride of place. FOREVER!

'Give me that!' Rudolph Trollyev snatched the certificate. 'There is only one prize in this competition. Ours! This certificate means nothing. Come, Desdemona! We are leaving!'

'No!' Desdemona shot double jets of

flame from her nostrils, creating a flurry
of activity as students with extinguishers
ran around putting out small fires. 'I may

be the world's most competitive ballerina dragon, but I won't be coached by someone who thinks it's fair to steal someone else's ideas. Promise me this will never happen again, or I'll move to New York to study with Madame Swirler!'

Madame Swirler gulped as she surveyed the scorched stage and the fires still burning, but she stiffened her spine and declared, 'If we can cope with a foolish unicorn, we can cope with a fire-breathing dragon. If you are unhappy where you are, Desdemona, you are always welcome to join us.'

'I might just do that,' Desdemona smiled.

Rudolph Trollyev stared at the two of them, stunned. My certificate fell from his slack fingers.

'I'll take that, thank you!' I scooped the award up from the floor and hugged it to my heart.

Rudolph Trollyev said a rude word.

Madame Swirler drew herself up to her full three feet and said firmly. 'Go now, Trollyev, before the judges decide to punish you for cheating!'

The great man shook his fist at us. 'I'll be back!' he bellowed as he stormed toward the exit. 'It is those unicorns who are cheats . . . Ouch!' he added as he barrelled into Frank, who was sprinting toward the stage, dressed in his leotard.

'Frank?' I asked as Rudolph Trollyev barged past him and out through the door.

'Can't talk. Got to run,' Frank scratched

his armpit excitedly. 'I'm competing! Arnie's been disqualified! The judges saw what he did during your routine. Don't worry, they said you won't be punished because you clearly weren't expecting it and it hurt rather than helped your routine. But Arnie's in trouble.' A smile lit up Frank's furry face.

I found myself smiling back. It was wonderful to see him so happy, and this meant I wouldn't have to tell Arnie off. The judges had already done it for me.

My smile grew even wider when Frank won the Modern Dance category. All that practice had paid off. Every single one of us from the New York School for Performing Arts finished in the top three, although I was the only one to get a special certificate. YAY, ME!

There was *another* cake waiting for me when we got back to school. Huge and chocolatey and melty, it

had `CHAMPION UNICORN` piped onto it in edible glitter. I didn't mind that you could see where the name 'Arnie' had been hurriedly smothered in frosting so they could write 'Louie' over the top. I was happy to share Champion Unicorn status. Arnie may have been a naughty unicorn today, but he was still my most dashing friend and I looked forward to competing with him again in the future.

Greetings, beloved parents,

Life continues to be as sparkly as ever. This week I was in a huge dance competition and I performed a Leaping Champion like a, well, Leaping Champion.

The judges were impressed! As it turned out, they were even more impressed by one of my fellow contestants. But that's OK. Desdemona the Dragon was a worthy winner and it was the best result for everyone. Partly because Desdemona gets a bit fire-breathy when things don't go her way, but mainly because she only got a trophy, whereas I got a certificate! How amazing it that? I'm waiting to get it framed and then I'll hang it in pride of place. Or I will when we can agree where 'pride of place' is. My friends think it's in the bathroom, just above the toilet. My friends are wrong.

The competition brought me closer to Madame Swirler and Arnie, but they're pretending nothing has changed. Sillies. Madame Swirler can't let people see she's not the grumpy-meany she pretends to be or no one will follow her orders, and Arnie is still cross about being told off. Frank, Danny and Miranda are right—he's not always kind—but it's just his way of protecting me. Because if he wasn't there, it would leave a gap for scarier rude people, like that horrible Rudolph Trollyev. So, yay, Arnie!

Love you more than cake,

Louie Xxxx

LOOK OUT FOR MORE ADVENTURES WITH LOUIE THE UNICORN.

Oscar Armelles was born in Spain, and almost from day one, could be found with a pen and paper in his hand, he loved to draw— anything and everything. As soon as he was old enough, he collected all his crayons and moved to America where he studied Commercial Art.

After graduating, he relocated to London and now he spends his time coming and going between London and Madrid.

He works mainly in digital format . . . although he is quite handy with watercolours too.

Rachel Hamilton studied at both Oxford and
Cambridge and has put her education to good use
working in an ad agency, a secondary school, a
building site, and a men's prison. Her interests
are books, films, stand-up comedy, and cake, and
she loves to make people laugh, especially when
it's intentional rather than accidental.

Rachel is currently working on the *Unicorn in
New York* series for OUP and divides her time
between the UK and the UAE, where she enjoys
making up funny stories for 7 to 13 year olds.

HERE ARE SOME OTHER STORIES THAT WE THINK YOU'LL LOVE.